# The Penguin Lady

by Carol A. Cole
illustrated by Sherry Rogers

3316
Penguin
Place

Penelope Parker lived on Penguin Place. She lived in
a neat little white house with black trim.
Short and stout, Penelope always wore her favorite
colors: black and white.
Penelope even waddled when she walked.

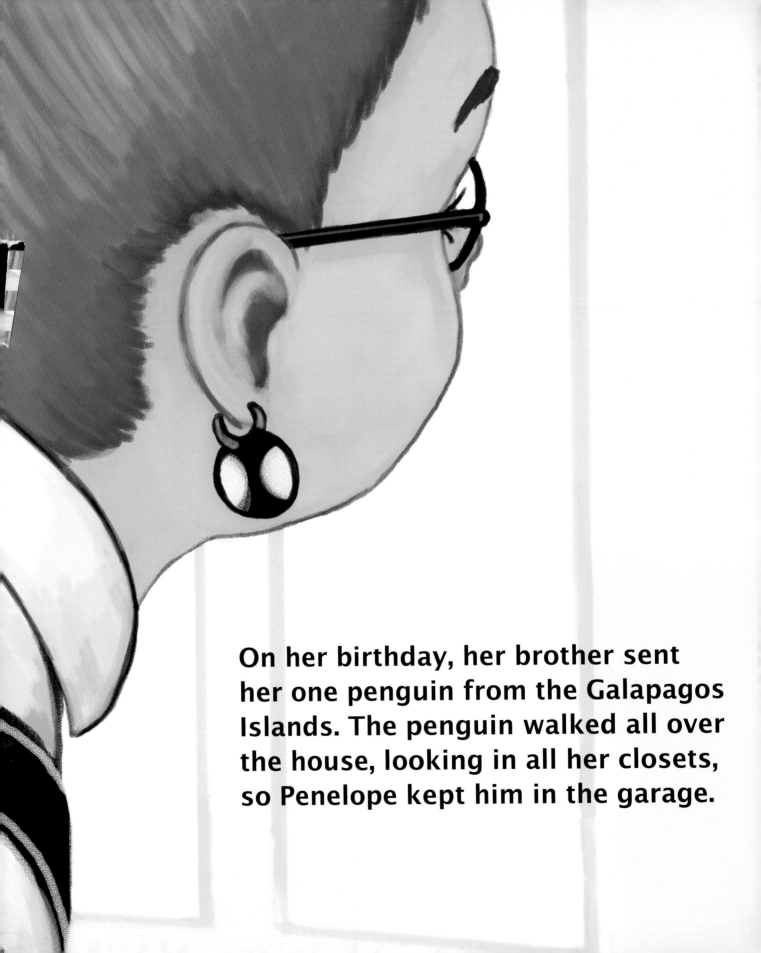

On her birthday, her brother sent her one penguin from the Galapagos Islands. The penguin walked all over the house, looking in all her closets, so Penelope kept him in the garage.

Then Penelope's sister gave her two Rockhopper penguins from Argentina. They liked to hop up onto her dining room table and sit next to the dishes.

One day Penelope opened her door and there were three Chinstrap penguins from Antarctica waddling across her front porch.

The local newspaper heard about them and sent a reporter to write a story about Penelope and the penguins. Her picture was on the front page of the newspaper.

When people read her story, they started sending Penelope orphaned penguins from all over the world. In the spring, four baby African penguins came and she put them in her air-conditioned attic.

Five Little Blue penguins from Australia lounged in the living room. They sat on all her chairs.

That summer, six Royal penguins from an island near Antarctica went swimming in the cool water in her backyard pond. When they came inside, they tracked muddy footprints all over Penelope's carpets.

One fall morning, Penelope found seven King penguins from the Falkland Islands standing in her kitchen.

One winter afternoon, eight Adelie penguins from Antarctica skated on her icy pond. That night, Penelope found their wet scarves piled on her favorite living room chair.

In the den, nine Macaroni
penguins from Argentina napped
on the piano. Penelope had to
tiptoe through her house so she
would not wake them.

Penguins paraded everywhere.

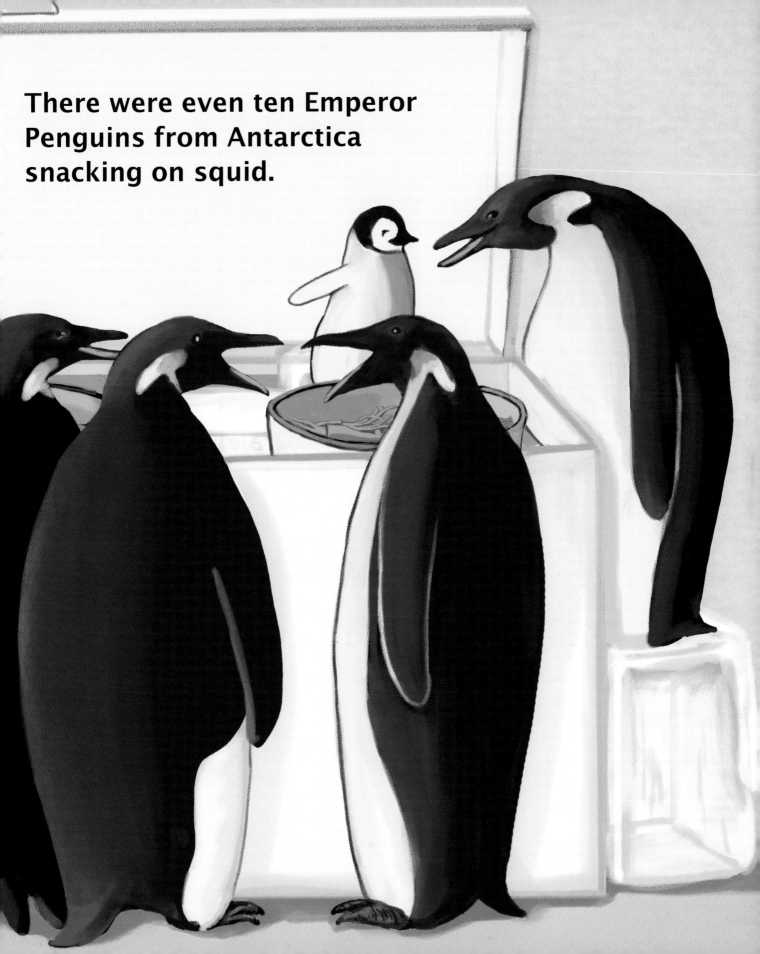

There were even ten Emperor Penguins from Antarctica snacking on squid.

Penguins were inside and outside of her house. Soon all the children on her street called her the penguin lady.

The penguins were loud and messy.

*This just won't do*, she thought. *I can't send them all back. What can I do with them?*

Penelope called her local zoo. "Do you need any more penguins?"
"Why yes," they said. "We do."

So, Penelope rented a large truck and helped all the penguins up the long ramp into the back of the truck. She drove them to the zoo where they were happy to meet other penguins.

All the penguins were gone. Penelope's house was quiet and empty. It was too quiet and she was very lonely.

Then, she saw a sign at her neighbor's house.
Dalmatian Puppies for Sale.

"I'll just take one." She smiled as she walked over.

# For Creative Minds

## Compare and Contrast Penguin Adaptations

Just as there are many breeds of dogs, there are different species of penguins. How are these penguins alike and how are they different?

Penguins are birds. Their wings look like flippers but the motion is the same as that of other birds flying through the air. They actually "fly" through the water instead of the air!

Rockhopper

Even though penguins spend most of their time in the water, they breathe oxygen from the air. They come up to the surface to breathe.

Some dive deep for food and can hold their breath for up to 15 minutes (Emperor). Others (Royal or Chinstrap) can only hold their breath for a minute or two.

Adelie

Their bodies are torpedo shaped to glide through the water.

Penguins have light chests and dark backs to hide (a type of camouflage called counter-shading) in the ocean. If seen from below, their light chest is hard to see in the light coming from above. Their dark back is hard to see from above against the dark depths of the ocean.

If warm on land, they'll hold out their flippers to cool down. Some also have patches near their eyes with no feathers where heat can escape. They can also release heat through their feet!

If cold, they'll tuck flippers close to their bodies.

They have muscular control of their feathers and can raise (to cool down) and lower them (to warm up) at will.

Royal

Macaroni

King

They use their webbed feet to steer while swimming.

Their ears are small holes covered with feathers. Their ears are in the same general place as our ears would be. They use sounds to find their mates and their young in crowded rookeries.

Penguins spend a lot of their time in the water but come onto ice or land to lay eggs and raise their young.

Penguins living in warmer climates nest in underground burrows, those in cooler climates make nests on the surface, and the largest (Emperor and King) penguins carry the eggs on their feet.

Penguin bills or beaks are used to catch and eat food and to defend themselves and their young.

They don't have teeth. Instead, they have fleshy spines on their tongue and inside of the beak to help keep slippery fish in their bills.

Penguins can see well in the water and on land.

Chinstrap

Penguin legs appear short because their body covers their legs almost to their ankles. That's why they waddle when they walk.

Most birds have light, hollow bones for flying. Penguins have heavy, dense bones for swimming.

African

All birds have feathers. Some penguins have 70-80 feathers per square inch to stay warm. Penguins that live in warmer climates have fewer feathers per square inch than penguins from colder climates.

The short feathers overlap.

The outer stiff part of the feather is waterproof.

The inner part of the feather is downy and traps warm air against the body—keeping the penguin warm in cold air and water.

A layer of fat under the feathers also provides some insulation.

Little Blue

one square inch

While on land, penguins use their sharp toe nails to dig nests and help move. Some penguins hop, jump, or even slide on their tummies to move!

Emperor          Galapagos

# Penguins of the World: True or False Questions

Which statements are true and which are false? Answers are upside down, below.

1. Polar bears are the biggest predator of most penguins.

2. Penguins only live in the southern hemisphere.

3. Some penguins live near the equator (shown as a red line on the map).

4. Some penguins live in Southern Africa.

5. Wild penguins live along rivers in North America.

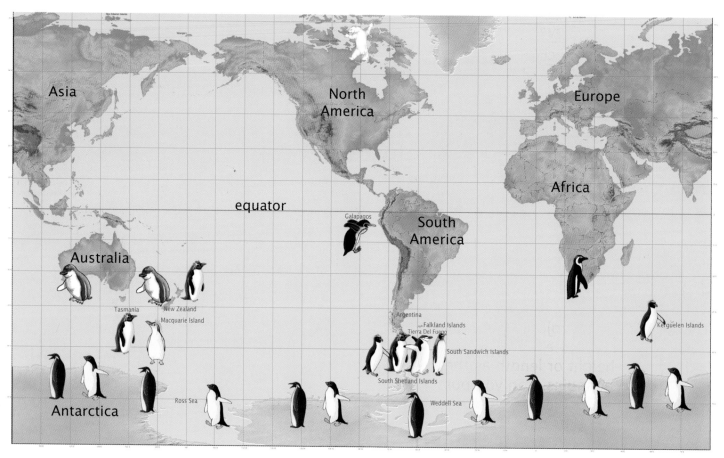

It isn't possible for individuals to have penguins as pets. You can help threatened or endangered penguins (and other animals) by "adopting" one with a donation to one of the many zoos, aquariums, or conservation programs that are working to care for these animals. Find more information and more learning activities on the book's homepage at www.SylvanDellPublishing.com and click on the book's cover.

| type of penguin | inches | centimeters |
|---|---|---|
| Adelie penguin | 20 | 51 |
| African penguin | 27 | 69 |
| Chinstrap penguin | 29 | 74 |
| Emperor penguin | 42 | 107 (1.1 m) |
| Galapagos penguin | 21 | 48 |
| King penguin | 35 | 89 |
| Little Blue penguin | 10 | 41 |
| Macaroni penguin | 28 | 71 |
| Royal penguin | 27 | 69 |
| Rockhopper penguin | 21 | 53 |

What measuring tool will you use?

How tall are you? Are there any penguins about your height?

Using yarn or string, measure and cut lengths to the size of each penguin and label them. If desired, go to the book's teaching activities (www.SylvanDellPublishing.com and click on the cover) to print and cut out penguin cards. Use the yarn to compare penguin sizes.

Find objects that are the same approximate height or length as the penguins. Can you put those objects in order by size?

How would you describe the penguins?

tall, taller, and tallest
short, shorter, shortest
big, bigger, biggest
small, smaller, smallest

To my husband Bob, and son Robert, for all of their support
and to Susan Wulf, the original Penguin Lady—CAC
To my wonderful son Joshua who has always loved penguins—SR
Thanks to illustrator Laurie Allen Klein for the use of her polar bear image from *Fur and Feathers*.

Thanks to Jean Pennycook, Penguin Education Specialist at Penguin Science; Heather Urquhart, Penguin Exhibit and Collection Manager and Erin Graichen, Education Programs Assistant at the New England Aquarium; and Tricia LeBlanc, Director of Education & Volunteers, at the Audubon Aquarium of the Americas for reviewing the For Creative Minds section for accuracy.

Library of Congress Cataloging-in-Publication Data

Cole, Carol A., 1950-
The penguin lady / by Carol A. Cole ; illustrated by Sherry Rogers.
p. cm.
ISBN 978-1-60718-527-7 (hardcover) -- ISBN 978-1-60718-536-9 (pbk.) -- ISBN 978-1-60718-545-1 (english ebook) -- ISBN 978-1-60718-554-3 (spanish ebook) 1. Penguins--Juvenile literature. I. Rogers, Sherry, ill. II. Title.
QL696.S473C653 2012
598.47--dc23
2011042375

Also available as eBooks featuring auto-flip, auto-read, 3D-page-curling, and selectable English and Spanish text and audio
Interest level: 003-008 Grade level: P-3 Lexile® 770L
Curriculum keywords: adaptations, anthropomorphic, counting, geography, map, species

Manufactured in China, December, 2011
This product conforms to CPSIA 2008
First Printing
Sylvan Dell Publishing
Mt. Pleasant, SC 29464